Wagons Ho!
A Diary of the Oregon Trail

Cynthia Mercati

Perfection Learning®

Cover and Inside Illustrations: Larassa Kabel

About the Author

Cynthia Mercati is a writer and a professional actress. She has written many plays for a children's theatre that tours and performs at various schools. She also appears in many of the plays herself.

Ms. Mercati loves reading about history and visiting historical places. When she writes a historical play or book, she wants her readers to feel like they are actually living the story.

Ms. Mercati also loves baseball. Her favorite team is the Chicago White Sox. She grew up in Chicago, Illinois, but she now lives in Des Moines, Iowa. Ms. Mercati has two children and one dog.

Image credits: Corbis pp. 29, 41; Nebraska Historical Society p. 15

Corel p. 49; National Archives and Records Administration pp. 8, 23, 24, 26, 27
Some images copyright ArtToday (www.arttoday.com)

Printed in the United States of America. For information, contact Perfection Learning® Corporation, 1000 North Second Avenue, P.O. Box 500, Logan, Iowa 51546-0500.
Phone: 1-800-831-4190 • Fax: 1-712-644-2392
ISBN 0-7891-5039-5 Paperback
ISBN 0-7807-9011-1 Cover Craft®

Contents

March 1, 1849

It's my tenth birthday today! This diary was my present from Ma and Pa. The pen I'm writing with was a present from my older brother. His name is Seth.

I have a sister too. Her name is Opal. She's only five. My name is Liza.

I will have many exciting things to write. In just nine days, we're leaving. Our family is going to start out for the Oregon Territory! We live in Illinois now.

I've never been farther away than ten miles from our farm. Now I'm going to travel clear across the country!

March 10, 1849

Pa sold our farm to buy a wagon. This is how we'll get to Oregon!

The wagon is called a **Conestoga**. It has high wooden boards on each side. Its wheels are rimmed with iron and painted red. They're as tall as Opal!

A thick white canvas cover tops our wagon. The cover stretches tightly between six wooden hoops. Ma and I sewed it ourselves!

I think our wagon looks like a boat. Opal thinks it looks like a loaf of bread!

Pa also bought six oxen to pull our wagon. They're **yoked** together in teams of two.

"Oxen don't go very fast," Pa said. "But they're strong! They'll be able to stand the trip much better than horses could."

Inside our wagon, we packed big sacks of flour and beans, a wooden washtub, and a big iron kettle. We also packed our sleeping **pallets** and quilts.

Ma, Opal, and I will sleep inside the wagon. Seth and Pa will sleep under it.

Our **grub** box is right up front. We can get to it quickly! Inside we packed slabs of bacon and jars of dried fruit and jelly. We also put in tin buckets filled with brown sugar, **lard**, coffee, and salt.

Ma's pots and pans hang on hooks on the outside of the wagon. Our water keg hangs there too.

Pa tied a big wooden box beneath the wagon. Inside are his tools and some spare wagon parts.

Ma cried when she found out there was no room for her china cabinet. And she couldn't take her rocking chair either.

My grandparents came to say good-bye the morning we left. All our neighbors came too.

Ma climbed up on the wagon seat. She took the reins in her hand. Opal climbed in next to her.

Seth tied up our two milk cows to the back of the wagon. He'll walk behind the wagon to guide the animals along. Pa will walk up front, next to the oxen.

I got into the back of the wagon. Daisy, our dog, jumped in beside me.

"Go safely," Grandmother said. "Once you're settled in Oregon, your grandfather and I are going to come out. We'll all live together on your big, new farm!"

Everyone was waving good-bye. I got a lump in my throat. It was hard to say good-bye to my friends.

For the first time, I felt scared and sad. We were leaving behind everyone and everything we knew.

And who knew what was waiting for us on the trail.

April 11, 1849

We have finally reached Independence, Missouri!

It's too dangerous for just one wagon to travel west alone. So people meet in Independence. There they form big **caravans** of wagons. These caravans are called *wagon trains*.

We have joined one of the trains. There will be 50 wagons in ours!

A man has been hired to head our wagon train. He's led people to Oregon several times before. His name is Tom McCullough. We all call him Captain McCullough.

The morning we left Independence, Captain McCullough got us up before sunrise! He sounded a blast on his trumpet.

Ma cooked us breakfast. Opal and I rolled up our bedding. Seth and Pa watered and fed the oxen. Then they hitched them to the wagon.

I picked up Daisy. Opal and I scrambled onto the seat next to Ma.

"Wagons ho!" Captain McCullough shouted. A cheer went up.

Pa called out to the lead oxen. "Gee, Bet! Gee, Blue!" He cracked his whip over the oxen's backs. They lurched forward. The wheels started turning. The pots and pans started clattering! We were on our way!

Pa smiled back at us. "Oregon or bust!" he shouted.

April 27, 1849

We're crossing the **Great Plains** now!

The sky is low and big. I feel like I could reach right up and grab a cloud!

All around us is tall prairie grass. It shines green-gold in the sun. It ripples like the waves of the ocean in the wind. Through this sea of grass, our wagons roll along like ships at sea.

Riding in the wagon is so bumpy. It makes my teeth rattle! Opal and I walk most of the time. Daisy runs next to us. There are lots of other children to talk to and play with.

All the spare oxen, saddle horses, and milk cows are at the back of the line. They call this the *cow column*. Seth and the older boys have to herd the cow column along.

Fifty wagons can really kick up dust! Captain McCullough has made a rule. First in line goes to the end of the line the next day. Then each day, you move up a place until you're in front again.

When the sun climbs high in the sky, we stop for lunch. We eat a cold meal of biscuits and jam. And we rest in the shade.

When we make camp for the night, we turn the wagons into a circle. On a good day, we make 12 miles!

There are hardly any trees on the plains. We have to use cow chips for our cooking fires! (That's a nice word for dried cow dung!) It's Opal's job to collect the cow chips in a big basket.

We always try to make camp by a river or stream. Opal and I have to fetch the water. Seth has to help Pa take care of the oxen.

Each night, I take down the bucket of axle grease from underneath the wagon seat. Then I grease each wagon wheel. I also have to check each spoke for cracks.

After supper, all the children run from wagon to wagon. Seth visits with his friends. The women talk a blue streak while mending. The men smoke their pipes and swap stories.

On Sundays, we rest. Captain McCullough reads a chapter from the Bible to all of us.

Ma bakes up a pie. That's her day to bake bread too.

It's also washing day for clothes and people! A line is strung between our wagon and the wagon next to us. That's where we hang the wash.

Then Ma heats up more water in the kettle. She pours it into the big tub. One by one, we climb in for our weekly baths. It sure feels good to get the dust off!

Some of the men have brought along their fiddles and banjos. I love it when they start playing around the campfire! Everyone claps and sings. Some people dance.

Pa and Ma even did a do-si-do! I usually grab Opal or one of my friends. We whirl around until we're dizzy and laughing! Daisy barks and jumps.

Sometimes to put myself to sleep, I quietly hum one of the fiddle tunes.

Buffalo gals, won't you come out tonight?
Come out tonight? Come out tonight?
Buffalo gals, won't you come out tonight?
And dance by the light of the moon!

May 10, 1849

Earlier, we were taking our noon rest. Suddenly, I heard thunder. But the sky was clear!

Captain McCullough came riding down the line.

"Swing the wagons in a circle!" he called out. "It's a buffalo stampede!"

A big, whirling cloud of dust was headed our way. Inside the dust cloud were the buffalo!

In what seemed like a few seconds, the wagons were in a circle. Ma grabbed Opal. I grabbed Daisy. Pa and Seth grabbed their guns from under the wagon seat. We all ducked under the wagon. Pa and Seth lay flat behind the wheels.

"We have to turn them!" Captain McCullough shouted.

The swirling dust drew ever nearer. Now I could see the great animals up close.

They were packed tight. Their shaggy heads were down. Their tails were in the air. The ground trembled under their hooves.

"Fire!" Captain McCullough shouted. The crack of rifles sliced the air.

The line of buffalo in the front of the pack fell to the ground. Then more went down. But more kept coming! It looked like they were going to plow right into our wagons!

"Fire!" Captain McCullough yelled. Again rifle shouts barked in the air.

I squeezed Dasiy so close she yelped. Opal was crying. Ma hugged her tight. Then she hugged me.

At Captain McCullough's order, the men fired again.

The gunshots were working. The line of shaggy animals split in the middle. They raced away from the pile of dead buffalo and past the wagons. Dust blew into our mouths and down our throats.

Finally, the last of the herd galloped by. The dust settled. The pounding of hundreds of hooves faded out.

Slowly, people crawled out from under their wagons.

Seth gave a long, low whistle. "That was a close call!"

June 23, 1849

We have passed Courthouse Rock and Chimney Rock. They're piles of red sandstone. We're in Wyoming Territory now!

We've also had our first bad storm. The sky turned black as midnight. Sheets of lightning lit up the land like fireworks!

The women crawled inside the wagons. The men stayed with the oxen. The rain seeped through our canvas cover. The wind blew so hard, it shook the wagon.

After the rain, the trail was a muddy mess! The wet brought the mosquitoes out something fierce. They swarmed over the oxen's heads and drove us crazy!

A few days later, we rolled into Fort Laramie. We're now 700 miles from Independence!

Fort Laramie is made of **adobe**. There's a big gate at the entrance. The walls are slit with loopholes for rifles to poke through.

Inside the fort, Ma bought flour and sugar at the **sutler's** shop. Pa had some tools repaired at the blacksmith's shop.

We saw many Sioux Indians at the fort. Some were there to trade. Lots of the men worked as horse **wranglers**.

Captain McCullough says Fort Laramie is the last outpost of civilization until we reach Oregon. His words make me shiver. There's no turning back now!

July 4, 1849

We timed it just right. We're camped near Independence Rock on our nation's birthday!

After we left Fort Laramie, the road was stony and steep. For a week, we traveled upward.

Then we saw Independence Rock! It was standing boldly against the sky!

The rock was named by an early party of traders who camped here on July 4. Captain McCullough scratched the name of our wagon train and the date into the famous rock.

We're in the mountains now! Tall cliffs rise up on either side of us. Many of the earlier wagon trains had to lighten their loads to make it up the trail. Scattered pieces of furniture are everywhere. We also see ovens, mirrors, plows, clothes, books. There was even a piano!

We are seeing more and more graves. One grave was marked with a wagon seat. On it were written the words "Oregon or Death." We passed that grave in silence.

July 18, 1849

Today as we creaked along, Captain McCullough fired a rifle shot. That's the signal for the train to stop.

Sitting tall in the saddle, Captain McCullough pointed to the valley ahead. Between the bare hills ran a stream.

"That's the **Continental Divide**," the captain called out.

"What does that mean?" Opal asked. Her eyes were wide.

"It means we're really, truly in the West," Pa answered. He sounded excited. "From here on in, all the rivers and streams will flow westward toward the Pacific Ocean!"

"Maybe that will help pull us along to Oregon!" Opal said.

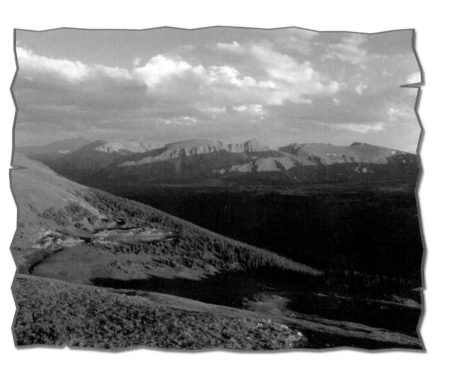

The next day we came to a long, steep hill. We stopped at the very top. The women and children scrambled down on our knees and our bottoms! The men lowered the wagons down on ropes, one at a time.

Pa and Seth locked the wheels of our wagon with poles. But still it slid like a sled! The oxen had to run at a swift clip to keep in front!

Several of the wagons overturned. One was so wrecked it had to be turned into a two-wheel cart.

I don't know which is worse. Going down the mountains or climbing up!

July 30, 1849

A party of Indian men visited our camp last night!

At the sight of them, the fiddles came to a stop. So did the banjos. So did all the people. We just stood and stared.

Their chests were bare. Their black hair was braided. They wore deerskin **leggings** and **moccasins**.

"They're not wearing war paint," Seth whispered to me.

The Oregon Trail

The family in this diary traveled from Illinois to Oregon. These are some of the important places along the Oregon Trail.

Independence, Missouri
Fort Kearny, Nebraska
Courthouse Rock
Chimney Rock
Scotts Bluff
Fort Laramie, Wyoming
Independence Rock
Devil's Gate
South Pass
Fort Bridger
Rocky Mountains

Continental Divide
Fort Boise
Blue Mountains
Cascade Mountains
Snake River
Rio Ronde Valley
Columbia River
Whitman's Mission
The Dalles
Willamette Valley
Oregon City

The family also went through many states and territories. Listed below are the years the territories they traveled through became states.

Missouri	1821
Kansas	1861
Nebraska	1867
Wyoming	1890
Idaho	1890
Washington	1889
Oregon	1859

Glossary

adobe	brick made of sun-dried earth and straw
caravan	group of vehicles and/or people traveling together
channel	stream of water between two close pieces of land
Conestoga	large canvas-topped wagon named after Conestoga, Pennsylvania, where the wagons were made

Continental Divide also called the backbone of a continent. In North America, the great ridge of the Rocky Mountains separates the streams and rivers flowing westward toward the Pacific Ocean from those flowing eastward toward the Atlantic.

current swiftest part of a stream or river

ford to cross water

Great Plains high grasslands. They include the western part of North Dakota, South Dakota, Nebraska, Kansas, and Oklahoma and the eastern part of Montana, Wyoming, Colorado, New Mexico, and Texas.

grub	food
lard	soft, white, solid or semi-solid fat. It usually comes from butchering a hog.
leggings	covering for the legs made of leather
lingo	language
moccasin	soft leather shoe
pallet	straw-filled mattress
parched	dried up; thirsty
plateau	high area of land with a flat surface
sutler	shopkeeper on an army post
wrangler	someone who takes care of horses

yoke   to hold together by a wooden bar. Usually two animals are held together at the neck so they can work as a team.

4/01

J MERCATI
Mercati, Cynthia.
Wagons ho!

There were several rushing, roaring streams to cross! The men had to tie ropes to the wagons and pull them across to the other side!

The nights are cold now. In the mornings, there's ice on the wagon wheels.

Sometimes we have to walk through snow. But it isn't deep. A cold wind blows all the time. Most of us have thrown our warm clothes away to lighten the wagons! By the time we make camp, we're chilled to the bone.

I pray we make it to Oregon before the first snowstorm. It could mean death for all of us if we're stranded in the mountains in a blizzard.

October 18, 1849

We made it! We're at the end of the trail! Today, creaking and groaning, our wagons rolled into Oregon City! People came out of their houses to say "Hello!"

Oregon truly is paradise! It's green everywhere! The air is soft. It's filled with the scent of pine trees.

Pa bought us a tent. We'll sleep in that until Pa and Seth can build us a cabin.

Before I crawled into the tent tonight, I sat outside to write these lines. Daisy was right next to me. Just like she's been every step of the way from Illinois.

I sure have learned a lot on this journey! I've seen a lot too. I reckon I couldn't have helped but grown up a lot!

I looked up at the sky. The Oregon sky! Then I gave Daisy a pat.

"We're home," I whispered.

THE OREGON TRAIL

- Oregon City
- Whitman's Mission
- Fort Boise
- Snake R.
- South Pass
- Devil's Gate
- Independence Rock
- Sweetwater R.
- Bear R.
- Fort Bridger
- Green R.
- Fort Laramie
- N. Platte R.
- Scotts Bluff
- Chimney Rock
- Courthouse Rock
- Platte R.
- S. Platte R.
- Fort Kearny
- St. Joseph
- Independence
- Fort Leavenworth

SCALE OF MILES

100 200 300 400 500